The Enormous Turnip

Alexei Tolstoy
Illustrated by Scott Goto

Green Light Readers
Harcourt, Inc.
San Diego   New York   London

www.HarcourtBooks.com

First Green Light Readers edition 2002
Green Light Readers is a trademark of Harcourt, Inc.,
registered in the United States of America and/or other jurisdictions.

Library of Congress Cataloging-in-Publication Data
Tolstoy, Aleksey Konstantinovich, graf, 1817–1875.
The enormous turnip/Alexei Tolstoy; illustrated by Scott Goto.
p. cm.
Summary: A cumulative tale in which the turnip planted by an old man grows
so enormous that everyone must help to pull it up.
[1. Turnips—Fiction. 2. Cooperativeness—Fiction.] I. Goto, Scott, ill. II. Title.
PZ7.T58En 2002
[E]—dc21 2001007733
ISBN 0-15-204585-6
ISBN 0-15-204584-8 pb

A C E G H F D B
A C E G H F D B (pb)

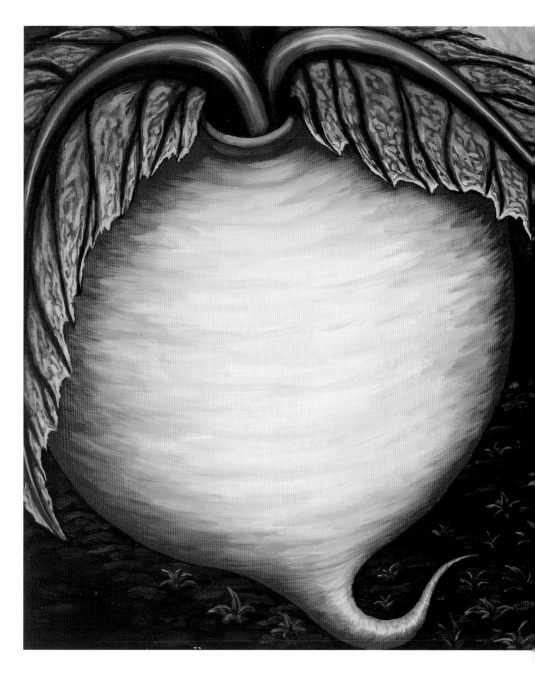

Once upon a time, an old man planted a little turnip. "Grow, grow, little turnip— grow sweet!" he said.

"Grow, grow, little turnip—grow strong!"
And the turnip grew up sweet and strong
and . . . *enormous.*

Then, one day, the old man tried to pull the turnip up. He pulled and pulled again, but he could not pull it up.

So, the old man called the old woman.

The old woman pulled the old man, the old
man pulled the turnip. They pulled and
pulled again, but they could not pull it up.

So, the old woman called her granddaughter.

The granddaughter pulled the old woman,
the old woman pulled the old man, the
old man pulled the turnip.

They pulled and pulled again, but they could not pull it up.
So, the granddaughter called the black dog.

The black dog pulled the granddaughter, the granddaughter pulled the old woman, the old woman pulled the old man, the old man pulled the turnip. They pulled and pulled again, but they could not pull it up.

So, the black dog called the cat.

The cat pulled the black dog, the black dog pulled the granddaughter, the granddaughter pulled the old woman, the old woman pulled the old man, the old man pulled the turnip. They pulled and pulled again, but *still* they could not pull it up....

So, the cat called the mouse.

The mouse pulled the cat, the cat pulled the black dog, the black dog pulled the granddaughter, the granddaughter pulled

the old woman, the old woman pulled the
old man, the old man pulled the turnip....

And up came the enormous turnip at last!

Meet the Illustrator and Author

Scott Goto has been drawing since he was a child. His love of art makes him work very hard to be the best artist he can be. He also loves learning about history and figures from history such as Tolstoy.

Alexei Tolstoy was a writer in Russia many years ago. He wrote children's tales as well as poems, plays, and stories for grown-ups. He also wrote science fiction stories. One of them is about people who visit the planet Mars.